P9-BUI-629

Also by Jean Echenoz from The New Press

Lightning

Running

Ravel

Piano

I'm Gone

Big Blondes

1914

A Novel

Jean Echenoz

Translated from the French
by Linda Coverdale

THE NEW PRESS

NEW YORK
LONDON

BRIDGEVIEW PUBLIC LIBRARY

The New Press gratefully acknowledges the Florence Gould
Foundation for supporting the publication of this book.

© 2012 by Les Éditions de Minuit
English translation © 2014 by The New Press
All rights reserved.

No part of this book may be reproduced, in any form,
without written permission from the publisher.

Requests for permission to reproduce selections from
this book should be mailed to: Permissions Department,
The New Press, 120 Wall Street, 31st floor, New York, NY 10005.

Originally published in France as _14_ by Les Éditions de
Minuit, 7, rue Bernard-Palissy, 75006, Paris, 2012
Published in the United States by The New Press, New York, 2014
Distributed by Perseus Distribution

LIBRARY OF CONGRESS CATALOGING-IN-PUBLICATION DATA
Echenoz, Jean.
[14. English]
1914 : a novel / Jean Echenoz ; Translated from
the French by Linda Coverdale.
pages   cm
"Originally published in France as 14 by Les Editions de
Minuit, 7, rue Bernard-Palissy, 75006, Paris, 2012."
ISBN 978-1-59558-911-8 (pbk. : alk. paper) — ISBN 978-1-59558-924-8
(e-book)   1. World War, 1914-1918 — France —
Fiction.   I. Title.   II. Title: Nineteen fourteen.
PQ2665.C5A61413 2013
843'.914—dc23
                  2013013990

The New Press publishes books that promote and enrich public
discussion and understanding of the issues vital to our democracy
and to a more equitable world. These books are made possible by
the enthusiasm of our readers; the support of a committed group of
donors, large and small; the collaboration of our many partners in the
independent media and the not-for-profit sector; booksellers, who often
hand-sell New Press books; librarians; and above all by our authors.
www.thenewpress.com

Composition by dix!
This book was set in Stempel Garamond
Printed in the United States of America

2   4   6   8   10   9   7   5   3   1

1914

I

SINCE THE WEATHER WAS so inviting and it was Saturday, a half day, which allowed him to leave work early, Anthime set out on his bicycle after lunch. His plans: to take advantage of the radiant August sun, enjoy some exercise in the fresh country air, and doubtless stretch out on the grass to read, for he'd strapped to his bicycle a book too bulky to fit in the wire basket. After coasting gently out of the city, he lazed easily along for about six flat miles until forced to stand up on his pedals while tackling a hill, sweating as he swayed from side to side. The hills of the Vendée in the Loire region of west-central France aren't much, of course, and it was only a slight rise, but lofty enough to provide a rewarding view.

As Anthime reached the crest of that eminence, a

rowdy gust of wind came up abruptly, almost carrying off his cap, and then buffeted his bicycle, a solid Euntes[1] he'd bought off a vicar now stricken with gout. Air currents that sudden, loud, and forceful in their onrush are rather unusual in that area in midsummer, especially on such a sunny day, and Anthime had to steady himself with one foot on the ground and the other on its pedal, with the bicycle slightly inclined beneath him, as he settled his cap firmly on his head in the whistling wind. Then he looked around at the countryside: a sprinkling of villages, an abundance of fields and pasturelands. Invisible yet also there, twelve or so miles to the west, breathed the ocean, on which Anthime happened to have ventured out some four or five times, occasions on which he had not been much help to his comrades, having no idea how to fish, although as an accountant, he had felt equipped to take on the always welcome responsibility of tallying up the mackerel, whiting, plaice, brill, and other flatfish back at the dock.

On that first day of August, standing alone on the hill, Anthime let his gaze linger over the panorama, taking in the five or six small market towns scattered below: clusters of low houses congregated around a belfry, linked by a slender network of roads on which the few automobiles were far outnumbered by oxcarts and draft horses hauling harvested grain. It was certainly a pleasant landscape, albeit one temporarily disrupted by that noisy, truly unseasonable eruption of wind rampaging everywhere within earshot, which forced Anthime to keep clutching his cap. The rushing air was all one could hear. It was four in the afternoon.

As Anthime glanced idly from one town to another, he noticed a phenomenon he'd never seen before. Atop every one of the belfries at the same moment, something had been set in motion, and this movement was tiny but steady: a black square and a white one, each following the other every two or three seconds, had begun regularly switching places like an alternating light, a binary blinking reminiscent of the automatic valves on certain machines back at the factory. Anthime watched but did not understand these mechanical pulses that seemed like trip levers, or winks launched from afar by a series of strangers.

Then, as abruptly as it had begun, the pervasive rumbling of the wind suddenly gave way to the noise it had masked until that moment: up in those church towers, the bells had in fact begun tolling all together, ringing out in a somber, heavy, and threatening disorder in which Anthime, although still too young to have attended many funerals, instinctively recognized the timbre of the tocsin, rung only rarely, the image of which had reached him separately before its sound.

The tocsin, given the world situation at the time, could mean only one thing: mobilization. Like everyone else but not taking the idea very seriously, Anthime had been rather expecting this, although he would never have imagined it happening on a Saturday. He listened quietly for less than a minute to the bells solemnly jostling one another, then straightened his bike and pushed off again, coasting all the way down the hill before turning toward home. Unnoticed by Anthime, his big book went sailing off the bicycle after a stiff bump, opening as it fell to lie forever alone at the roadside, facedown on the chapter entitled "Aures Habet et non Audiet." [2]

Entering the town, Anthime began to see people leaving their houses to gather in groups before converging on the Place Royale. The men seemed excited, on edge in the heat, turning to call to one another, gesturing broadly but with seeming confidence. Anthime dropped off his bicycle at home before joining the general movement now flowing in from every direction toward the main square, where a smiling crowd milled around waving bottles and flags, gesticulating, dashing about, leaving barely enough space for the horse-drawn vehicles already arriving laden with passengers. Everyone appeared well pleased with the mobilization in a hubbub of feverish debates, hearty laughter, hymns, fanfares, and patriotic exclamations punctuated by the neighing of horses.

Across the square and beyond that animated throng red-faced with sweat and fervor, Anthime spotted Charles on the corner of the Rue Crébillon, by a silk merchant's shop, and tried at a distance to catch his eye. Unsuccessful in this, he began making his way toward him through the crowd. Apparently remaining aloof from events, dressed as in his office at the factory in a close-fitting suit and a narrow, light-colored tie, Charles considered the crush of people without any visible emotion, wearing his Rêve Idéal camera from Girard &

Boitte slung around his neck, as usual. Advancing toward him, Anthime had to steel and calm himself at the same time, a paradoxical yet necessary procedure he followed to master the intimidating uneasiness he felt in the presence of Charles, no matter what the occasion. The other man faced him for barely a second before looking down at the signet ring Anthime wore on his pinkie.

Hmm, said Charles, that's new. And you're wearing it on your right hand, well, well. They're usually worn on the left. I know, agreed Anthime, but it isn't a question of style, it's because my wrist hurts. Indeed, said Charles condescendingly, and it doesn't bother you when you shake someone's hand. I shake so few hands, observed Anthime, and as I told you, it's for those pains I get in my right wrist, it relieves them. The ring's a bit heavy but it seems to work. It's a magnetic thing, if you like. Magnetic, repeated Charles with a trace of a smile, puffing a trace of a humph out his nose, shaking his head while shrugging one shoulder and looking away—and completing these five actions in a single second, leaving Anthime feeling once again humiliated.

So, began Anthime, trying to carry on by jerking

his thumb toward a group waving signs, what do you think of this. It was inevitable, replied Charles, closing one of his cold eyes to clap the other one to his view-finder, but it won't last longer than two weeks at the most. Of that, Anthime ventured to remark, I'm not so sure. Well, said Charles, tomorrow we'll see.

2

AND THE NEXT MORNING, they all found themselves at the barracks. Anthime had arrived there quite early, having joined his fishing and café comrades along the way: Padioleau, Bossis, and Arcenel, that last mumbling complaints about celebrating the occasion too long into the wee hours the night before, stirring up hemorrhoids and a hangover. Padioleau, slightly built, a touch timid, thin-faced with a waxy complexion, had nothing of the sturdy presence of a butcher's boy even though that was, in fact, his profession, whereas Bossis, not content with possessing the physique of a knacker, actually was one. As for Arcenel, he was a saddler, a craft that pre-supposes no particular habitus. In any case, each in his own way, these three took a great interest in animals, had seen lots of them, and were going to encounter a great many more.

Like all the first men to show up, they were rewarded with a uniform in their size, whereas Charles, eternally haughty and indifferent, arrived late enough that morning to earn himself an ill-fitting one at first, but when he protested disdainfully, fussing arrogantly over his position as a deputy plant manager, others— Bossis and Padioleau, as it turned out—were forced to give up some red trousers and a greatcoat that were apparently acceptable to such a leading citizen, despite his stoically disgusted expression. So Padioleau found himself utterly swamped by his reassigned greatcoat while Bossis never did manage, for as long as he had left to live, to get used to those pants.

Of medium height with an ordinary face, rarely smiling, sporting a mustache like just about all the men of his generation, twenty-three years old, wearing his new uniform with no more panache than he had in his everyday clothes, Anthime had intended to go speak to Charles: twenty-seven, no less poker-faced and mustached but more dashing, taller, more slender, turning his composed and icy gaze upon the world, apparently more bent than ever on remaining cool and distant, refusing to acknowledge anyone at all of lesser status, and doubtless Anthime in particular. Who therefore decided to forget it and rejoined his companions, if only to calm down Bossis, who was grumbling about his pants. Turning anyway to look back at Charles, Anthime saw him extract a cigar from a case he seemed about to slip back into his pocket but instead, pausing, he selected another cigar and offered it discreetly to the closest officer. Then Anthime watched him photograph that officer the way he had been photographing, for months now, everything he could get his hands on, perfecting his skills in that department to the point of having recently seen some of his pictures published in magazines like *Le Miroir* and *L'Illustration*, which accepted material from amateurs.

In the days that followed, everything moved fairly swiftly at the barracks. After the arrival of the last reservists, the territorials came in, nonprofessional soldiers organized on a local basis for home defense, old fellows between thirty-four and forty-nine years of age who were immediately called upon to stand drinks all around, and indeed, from Monday to Thursday those rounds came one after the other at a fast clip: by the end of the evening, everyone was somewhat the worse for wear. Then matters took a more serious turn when the squadrons were made up: Anthime found himself assigned to the 11th Squadron of the 10th Company, going up the chain to the 93rd Infantry Regiment, the 42nd Infantry Brigade, the 21st Infantry Division, and the 11th Army Corps of the 5th Army. Serial number 4221. The ammunition was distributed with the iron rations[3]—the emergency food supplies—and that evening, everyone again hit the bottle pretty hard. The next day was when they began to feel like soldiers: in the morning, the regiment drilled in formation for the first time, then passed in review before the colonel on the barracks square and paraded through the town that afternoon, since it was not yet time for them to leave on the troop train.

It was rather fun, that parade, with each man trying to walk tall in his uniform and look straight ahead. The 93rd marched along the avenue and then the main streets, lined by townspeople who weren't stingy with their tossed flowers, cheers, and shouts of encouragement. Charles had of course wangled himself a spot in the front line of the procession; Anthime was in the middle of the regiment, grouped with Bossis, still ill at ease in his trousers, along with Arcenel, complaining constantly about his rear end, and Padioleau, whose mother had had time to take in the greatcoat at the shoulders and shorten the sleeves. As Anthime marched along trading muttered jokes with his pals, trying all the while to keep stepping out smartly, he thought he noticed Blanche on the left sidewalk of the avenue. At first he took her for a lookalike but then, no, it was she, Blanche, all dressed up in a lightweight pink skirt and summery mauve blouse. To protect herself from the sun she was sheltering under a big black umbrella while the troop was sweating along in cadence in their new kepis, quite tight at the temples, plus the knapsack strapped on according to regulations and which, that first day, did not weigh too heavily yet on the collarbones.

As he'd expected, Anthime had first seen Blanche smile proudly at Charles's martial bearing and then, as he drew abreast of her in turn, he was not a little surprised when she gave him a different kind of smile, more serious and even, he felt, a trifle more emotional, pronounced, sustained, well who knows, exactly. He had neither seen nor tried to see how Charles—with his back to him, in any case—had reacted to her smile but he, Anthime, had responded only with a look, the shortest and longest one possible, forcing himself to invest it with the least amount of expression while at the same time suggesting the maximum: a novel approach, doubly paradoxical this time and which, as he strove to keep in step, was no small undertaking. After they'd filed past Blanche, Anthime preferred not to look at any more people.

At the station early the next morning, Blanche was there again, on the platform among the crowd waving little flags, as some boys chalked ON TO BERLIN on the flanks of the locomotive and a four- or five-man brass band did its best with the national anthem. Hats, scarves, bouquets, hankies, waved every which way as baskets of provisions passed through the train's windows, hugs enveloped children and old folks, couples embraced, and tears fell on the railcar steps—as one can see today in Paris in Albert Herter's vast mural in the Hall Alsace of the Gare de l'Est.[4] On the whole, however, people smiled confidently because it would all be over quickly, apparently, so everyone would be back soon—and from a distance, as Charles held Blanche in his arms, Anthime saw her gaze over his shoulder and once again direct that same look at him. Then it was time to get on the train and barely a week after his little bicycle excursion, after heading northeast from Nantes at six o'clock on Saturday morning, Anthime arrived up in the Ardennes on Monday in the late afternoon.

3

On Sunday morning, Blanche awoke in her bedroom on the second floor of an imposing residence of the kind belonging to notaries, deputies, public officials, or plant managers: the Borne family runs the Borne-Sèze factory, and Blanche is their only daughter.

A strangely discordant atmosphere reigns in this albeit peaceful and orderly room. Framed local scenes—barges on the Loire, fishermen's lives on the island of Noirmoutier—adorn the slightly off-center flowered wallpaper, and the furniture bespeaks an effort toward woodlands diversity worthy of an arboretum: a mirrored walnut *bonnetière*,[5] a writing desk of oak, a mahogany chest of drawers with fruitwood veneer, while the bed is of wild cherry, the armoire of yellow pine. So, an unusual ambience, and one ponders whether it arises from the mismatched edges—unexpected in what should be a meticulously appointed bourgeois house— of this faded wallpaper in which the bouquets are wilting as well, or from the astonishing variety of furniture woods: one wonders at first how so many different materials can get along together. And then one quickly senses that they do not get along at all, they cannot even stand one another, which probably explains the strange ambience: that must be it.

Until Blanche gets up, this furniture waits patiently to play its role. The night table—of beech—bears a lamp resting atop a few books, including Marc Elder's *The People of the Sea,* a volume Blanche dips into occasionally, not so much for its stalwart capture of the previous year's Goncourt Prize from a field including Marcel Proust as for her family's friendship with the author, a local man whose real name is Marcel Tendron, and because this work reminds her of past Sunday excursions into the countryside to see the fishermen of Noirmoutier or barges moored for the estuary fishing of eels, lampreys, and elvers at Trentemoult, a village of fishermen and sailors on the left bank of the Loire.

Once out of bed the first thing Blanche did was

decide what she would wear, selecting from the *bon-netière* a light short-sleeved blouse of batiste, from the armoire a suit of gray tweed, then stockings and under-garments from the drawer of the chest, on which a cou-ple of perfume bottles sit forgotten. Hesitating between two pairs of shoes—lower or higher heels?—but not over her hat, a rice-straw affair trimmed with black vel-vet. After a scant hour in the bathroom, freshly bathed and dressed, she consulted the mirror on the *bonnetière* with a critical eye, smoothing a lock of hair, adjusting a pleat. As she left her bedroom she passed the writing desk, which had played no part in this morning's activ-ity; the desk is used to this, serving simply as a reposi-tory for the letters Charles and Anthime each regularly sends separately to Blanche and which lie bound by rib-bons of contrasting colors in two different drawers.

Ready now, Blanche went quietly downstairs and on her way through the hall to the front door, made a detour to avoid the dining room. There—harsh grating of the bread knife against crust, clinking of teaspoons amid the aroma of chicory—her parents were finish-ing their breakfast: little audible conversation between Eugène and Maryvonne Borne; rumbling ingestion from the factory owner, melancholy sighs from the factory owner's wife. Pausing at the front door by the wicker umbrella stand lined with waterproof canvas, Blanche chose a parasol of checked cretonne.

Once outside, she went toward the street entrance to the garden, the main walk of which—white gravel, carefully raked—branches out into lesser paths leading past the shrubberies, pond, arbors, and ornamental trees, including a worn-out palm that has been holding on for too long in this climate. Blanche has also avoided, but with fewer precautions, the hunched figure of the lame gardener—who is as deaf as the palm tree and busy watering the grass borders and flower beds—by simply walking more softly on the crunching gravel until reaching the cast-iron front gates.

Outside, the sounds of Sunday: everything is quieter than on weekdays, the way it is on any Sunday but it's not just that, not the same silence as usual, it's as if a residual echo has remained of the clamor and fanfares and ovations of recent days. Early this morning the oldest municipal employees still left in town finished sweeping up the last bedraggled bouquets, rumpled rosettes, tattered banners, and dried-out tear-stained handkerchiefs before hosing down the pavements. A few errant items have been placed in the lost-and-found department: a cane, two torn scarves, and three dented hats, tossed in the air with patriotic fervor and whose legitimate wearers have not yet appeared but are awaited in due course.

The atmosphere is also calmer because there are fewer people in the streets, and fewer young men in particular, or only ones so young that, convinced along with everyone else that this conflict will be brief, they're ignoring it and don't let it bother them. The few boys of her age Blanche encounters, who all seem more or less unwell, have been declared unfit for military service, at least temporarily; this might change in the future but they're not concerned about that either. The near-sighted, for example, currently exempt and protected by their glasses, never dream for an instant that they might be traveling with them one day on a train to the east, with a spare pair of spectacles, if possible. Likewise for the deaf, the flat-footed, those with nervous complaints. As for malingerers or men who, confident of their connections and officially "unfit," don't even bother to pretend, they prefer not to show themselves too much for the moment. The brasseries are deserted, their waiters have disappeared: it's up to the bosses to sweep their terraces and doorsteps themselves. The dimensions of this town drained almost empty of its men thus seem to have expanded: other than women, Blanche sees only old fellows and kids, whose footsteps sound hollow on a stage too large for them.

4

HADN'T REALLY BEEN THAT bad either, in the train, just uncomfortable. Sitting on the floor they had devoured their provisions, sung every possible song, and booed Kaiser Willy, drinking right along. In the twenty or so stations where the convoy had stopped, they hadn't been allowed off the train to take a look at the towns but—through windows open to air that was too hot, speckled with sparks, almost solid with a heat coming from who knew where anymore, August or the locomotive and probably both, piling up—at least they'd seen a few airplanes. Some of these, in flight, were crossing a perfectly smooth sky at various altitudes, following or encountering and passing by one another bound on some unimaginable mission; others were sitting around higgledy-piggledy, surrounded by men in leather helmets, on requisitioned fields lying next to the tracks.

The men had heard about them, looked at photos in the newspaper, but no one had yet actually seen any of them, these seemingly fragile airplanes, except Charles no doubt—always au courant with everything, he had even climbed inside or rather onto a few, since there were no cabins yet—but Anthime had looked for him in vain among his fellow passengers. The landscape having about exhausted its attractions, Anthime turned aside to find some other way to kill time: cards, at that point, seemed just the thing, and along with Bossis and Padioleau—Arcenel being still too disabled by his derrière to join them—Anthime managed to claim a corner to launch a game of manille[6] beneath the soon-empty canteens swinging by their straps from hooks.

Then, since three-handed manille was a tricky business, and with Padioleau falling asleep as Bossis grew drowsy as well, Anthime shut down the game to go exploring in the neighboring cars, looking vaguely for Charles without really wanting to see him, assuming he was off by himself, contemptuous as always of his fellow men but surrounded by them of necessity. Well, not at all: Anthime eventually spotted him comfortably installed by a window in a car with seats, taking pictures of the landscape in the company of a clutch of noncommissioned officers whose photos he was also taking, along with their addresses so he could send them their portraits later on. Anthime wandered off.

In the Ardennes, they'd hardly gotten off the train, hardly had the time to get used to this new landscape of dense forests and rolling hills, hadn't even learned the name of this village where their first camp was or how long they'd be there—when some sergeants lined the men up and the captain made a speech at the foot of the cross on the main square. They were a little tired, didn't feel much like muttering jokes to one another anymore but they listened to it, this speech, standing at attention looking at trees of a kind they'd never seen before, as the birds in these trees began to tune up, getting ready to play taps in the twilight.

The captain, named Vayssière, was a puny young man with a monocle, a curiously ruddy complexion, and a limp voice: Anthime had never seen him before, and his morphology gave no hint as to why or how he could ever have desired and pursued a combative vocation. You will all return home, Captain Vayssière promised in particular, raising his voice to the limit of its power. Yes, we will all go home to the Vendée. One vital point, however. If a few men do die while at war, it's for lack of hygiene. Because it isn't bullets that kill, it is uncleanliness that is fatal and which you must combat first of all. So wash, shave, comb your hair, and you will have nothing to fear.

After that pep talk, as the men were breaking ranks, Anthime happened to find himself next to Charles, near the field kitchen just being set up. Charles did not seem any more inclined than usual or than in the train to chat about the war or the factory, but regarding the latter, well, he clearly couldn't slip off down one of his hallways claiming urgent correspondence to attend to as he'd always done before, so he was forced to deal with Anthime's concerns. And they were both dressed alike now, which always helps communication. About the factory, Anthime asked anxiously, what are we going to do? I have Mme. Prochasson to take care of everything, explained Charles, she has the files in hand. It's the same for you, you have Françoise in the accounts department, you'll find everything in order when you get back. But when's that, wondered Anthime. It won't take long, Charles insisted, we'll be back for the September orders. Hmm, said Anthime, we'll see about that.

The men drifted around the camp a bit, long enough to inquire about the resources available in the area. Some fellows were already complaining that they'd found nothing to eat, no beer or even matches, and the price of wine, sold by locals who'd quickly discovered how to profit from the situation, was now exorbitant. Trains could be heard going by in the distance. As for the field kitchen, nothing to be hoped for there until it was completely operational. Since their travel provisions were all gone, after sharing some cold monkey meat and murky water they went to bed.

5

Leaving behind the serried ranks of buildings, the squares with their old houses huddled together, Blanche went farther and farther away from the center of town along thoroughfares that were more open and airy, with somewhat unusual, almost eccentric, and certainly less regimented architecture: these houses in a greater variety or even absence of styles breathed more freely, set back from the street, and all had some form or other of garden around them. Continuing along her way, Blanche passed in front of Charles's residence and then Anthime's, now equally deserted.

Charles's house: beyond an ornate front gate concealing a garden one felt was flourishing, with well-tended flowers and lawns, a path led to a flagstone terrace set off by pillars flanking a double front door of polychrome stained glass, enthroned atop three steps. From the street, one could just make out at some distance the yellow and blue granite facade: tall, narrow, and, like its owner, tightly shut up. Three stories, with a balcony on the second floor.

Anthime's: this was a single-story house set closer to the street, with a roughcast facade, lower and more compact, as if a residence, like a dog, absolutely had to be homothetic to its master. Less well hidden by a front gate—ajar—made of ill-joined planks covered with flaking white paint, the property was a smaller and poorly defined zone of weeds bordered by some attempts at vegetable gardening. To enter Anthime's home one had next to cross a cracked slab of concrete ornamented solely by some very distinct and canine paw prints—from an animal therefore probably none too light on its feet—left in the fresh cement on the distant day it was poured. The only memorial to the defunct animal remained these impressions, at the bottom of which had accumulated an earthy grit, an organic residue in which other weeds, of a smaller format, were struggling to grow.

Blanche had given these two domiciles only a

passing glance as she walked on toward the factory, a continent-sized heap of dark brick as ponderous as a fortress, isolated from the neighborhood by timid little streets running all around it, as a moat encircles a château. Ordinarily gaping, the enormous main entrance, a maw that periodically engulfed fresh masses of laborers only to regurgitate them utterly exhausted, was on this Sunday closed as tightly as a savings bank. On the circular pediment atop this entrance moved the hands of a gigantic clock, with BORNE-SÈZE spelled out by huge letters in high relief. Below, on the gate, hung a sign bearing two words: NOW HIRING. This factory made footwear.

All kinds of footwear: shoes for men, women, and children, boots, bootees, and ankle boots, Gibsons and Oxfords, sandals and moccasins, boxing shoes, slippers, mules, orthopedic and safety shoes, even the recently invented snow boot, and not forgetting the *godillot*, that military boot named after its creator, the discoverer of—among other marvels—the difference between the left foot and the right. Everything for the feet at Borne-Sèze: from galoshes to pumps, from buskins to high heels.

Pivoting on hers, Blanche walked around the factory toward an isolated structure of the same dark brick, apparently one of the plant's outbuildings. DR. MONTEIL, announced a copper plate beneath the door knocker, and hardly had she knocked when this practitioner appeared: rather tall, stooped, with a florid complexion, dressed in gray, looking fiftyish enough—just above the age limit for territorial soldiers—to have narrowly escaped the mobilization. The Bornes had been his patients for a long time when Eugène had asked Monteil to become the factory's physician—participating in the selection and orientation of new hires, offering consultations and emergency care, giving the odd lecture on industrial hygiene—and although Monteil had immediately cut back on his private practice, he had remained the family doctor for the Bornes and three other local dynasties, while retaining as well his seat on the municipal council. Dr. Monteil knew quite a few people and had connections just about everywhere, even in Paris. He had taken care of Blanche ever since her infancy, so she had come to consult him in his capacity as both doctor and public official.

To the official she spoke of Charles, gone with the

others toward the northeastern border, no one knew exactly where. When she spoke of a possible intervention, with the hope of an assignment other than the infantry, Monteil asked what she might have in mind. Well, suggested Blanche, aside from the factory, which takes up all his time, Charles is very interested in aviation and photography. Perhaps there might be something to be done along those lines, replied Monteil. The Air Service, I believe they call it now. Let me think about this, I might have someone in mind at the ministry, I'll keep you informed.

To the general practitioner she explained her situation, showing him her figure under her clothing, and the exam did not take long. Palpation, two questions, diagnosis: definitely, declared Monteil, you are. And when will it be, asked Blanche. The beginning of next year, he figured, and I'd say toward the end of January. Blanche said nothing, looked at the window—where nothing was going on or past, not the slightest bird or anything—and then at her hands as she placed them on her belly. And you plan to keep it, of course, remarked Monteil to break the silence. I don't know yet, said Blanche. Otherwise, he said more softly, there would always be a way. I know, said Blanche, there's Ruffier. Yes, said Monteil, although, not since the other day, he went off like everyone else but we're talking about two weeks, it will all be over quickly. Or else his wife could always be of service. Silence again and then no, said Blanche, I think I will keep it.

6

So, CHARLES HAD FIGURED, in that August sunshine three months ago: it will all be over in two weeks. Which Monteil had said in turn, because many had believed this back then. Except that two weeks later, four weeks later, after more and still more weeks, once it had begun to rain and the days had grown ever shorter and colder, events did not turn out as expected.

Still, on the day after their arrival in the Ardennes, things hadn't looked that dire. One couldn't complain about the weather, a trifle cooler than in the Vendée; the air was pure, crisp, and the men felt good, on the whole. Of course they'd been treated to drilling that morning with packs and gear, but this is fairly normal in the army, it's practically like playing a game. Charles was still keeping some distance between himself and

Anthime—and increasingly vice versa—but they had
smiled together at Bossis and his jokes, then laughed un-
kindly when a mean lieutenant made fun of Padioleau's
way of presenting arms during the drill. Afterward,
everyone except those who didn't know how had written a few postcards made more festive by a magical find,
an aperitif: Byrrh[7] with a dribble of lemon syrup but
not seltzer, unfortunately, only plain water, followed by
a lunch that wasn't so terrible and which they'd even
managed to cap with a little nap before going off late
that afternoon to buy some plums at a local garden.

It was the day after that when things came into
clearer focus: three weeks of almost constant marching.
Along roads that grew dusty as the dew dried, the men
set out almost every morning at four o'clock, sometimes
cutting across fields, never stopping for even a moment.
After four or five days, when the weather turned hot
and muggy, they were allowed a small respite every half
hour from the midpoint of the march on, but men soon
began collapsing all the time, especially among the reservists, with Padioleau dropping more often than the
others. When they halted for the night, with everybody

worn-out, no one wanted to cook so they'd open cans of bully beef without much to wash it down.

For it had dawned on them only too quickly how impossible it was to get wine there, or indeed any beverage except a bit of raw alcohol, on occasion, at a price now increased fivefold by the distillers in the villages through which they passed, where the locals profited greedily from the golden opportunity presented by thirsty troops. This situation would soon change, when headquarters grasped the advantage presented by men properly supplied with drink, since inebriation damped down fear, but things had not yet come to that. Meanwhile and increasingly frequently they still saw a few airplanes passing overhead, it was a distraction, and then the heat began to abate.

Aside from the merchants, however, who also had tobacco, hard sausages, and jams on offer, in the villages but also at the edges of fields along their route small groups of country people gathered to cheer the troops on and surprisingly often, from simple generosity, to give them flowers, fruit, bread, and whatever wine they still had. Sometimes the people of these backwaters had seen the enemy arrive out of nowhere, and sometimes they'd been forced to pay a great deal of money to keep from being bombarded. Trudging along, the soldiers would examine the women gathered by the roadside, noticing some young and pretty ones on occasion. Over toward the town of Écordal, one of them, neither young nor pretty, tossed them some religious medals.

More and more, the men were also passing through certain villages abandoned by their inhabitants or even in ruins, destroyed or burned, perhaps, for not having paid any tribute. The cellars of empty houses had often been looted of everything but the occasional few bottles of Vichy water. The deserted streets were littered with divers damaged articles, and for the most part the troop left them lying there: unused cartridges discarded by a passing company, scattered clothing and linens, pots without handles, empty bottles, a birth certificate, a sick dog, a ten of clubs, a broken shovel.

What also happened was that the situation came into yet clearer focus when rumors began circulating, especially about spying: a traitorous teacher had been surprised, it seemed, in this or that sector, preparing to blow up a bridge. It was even possible, supposedly, that these spies had turned up near Saint-Quentin: two of them had been seen tied to a tree, convicted of having spent the entire night passing information to the enemy via lantern signals, and then as the troop drew closer, they saw the colonel kill them point-blank with his revolver. One evening, as it happened, after they'd been on the march for two weeks, they received orders to blacken their mess tins to reduce their visibility. Unsure how to proceed, Anthime looked at what the others were doing, each in his own way, then coped with a little paste of dirt and boot polish. Yes, it was all definitely becoming clear.

Two weeks after the expedition had set out was also when Anthime suddenly realized that he never saw Charles anymore. Risking a razzing, he spent two days going up and down the company's ranks as they tramped along, hoping at least to catch a glimpse of him but succeeding only in exhausting himself even further. Then he started asking around, questioning tight-lipped and supercilious noncoms at first, until a more cooperative sergeant told him one evening that Charles had been transferred, no one knew where, a military secret. Anthime hardly reacted at all, he was so dead on his feet.

In the evenings, moreover, it was often quite a challenge to find a place to sleep where the troop had halted. Since there wasn't much room for the men in the villages, half the company was usually obliged to try sleeping outdoors; when a village was deserted, the luckiest men camped in abandoned houses, where there might still be a bit of furniture and even sometimes beds, but no bedding. Most of the time, though, they'd fix up sleeping spots in the gardens or out in the fields of beets or oats or in the woods, beneath shelters they constructed from branches or in a providential haystack, and once in an abandoned sugar factory. Wherever they wound up, they never found comfort yet fell asleep fast.

In spite of their fatigue, before turning in for the night they tended to routine chores: laundry duty, inspection of shoes and feet. For distraction and relaxation, some men played cards, dominos, checkers, leapfrog, and even organized high-jump competitions or sack races. Arcenel, however, would simply carve his name with his knife, and Anthime just his initials along with the day's date, on a tree or a wooden roadside cross. After the evening meal, the men would sleep, then set out again at the bugler's call after harnessing themselves up, slinging their rifles, musette bags, and canteens over their shoulders, with cartridge pouches at their belts, but only after first hoisting onto their backs the 1893 model knapsacks nicknamed the Ace of Diamonds, made of a square wooden frame covered with a thick envelope of blackboard-green or licorice-brown canvas.[8] The men buckled them on with a pair of shoulder straps, each made of two pieces of leather joined by a brass rivet.

Empty, the pack weighed only one and a third pounds. It quickly grew heavier, however, with a first lot of regulation equipment carefully arranged inside and consisting of alimentary matériel (bottles of strong mint extract, coffee substitute, tins and sachets of sugar and chocolate, water bottles and cutlery of tin-plated iron, pressed iron mug, can opener, penknife), clothing (long and short underpants, cotton handkerchiefs, flannel shirts, suspenders, puttees), cleaning and maintenance products (clothes and shoe brushes, and for the weapons, tins of grease, polish, plus extra laces and buttons, sewing kit with round-tipped scissors), first-aid and toiletry articles (individual bandages, absorbent cotton wool, towel, mirror, soap, razor and strop, shaving brush, toothbrush, comb), as well as personal items (tobacco and rolling papers, matches and tinder-box, flashlight, nickel silver and aluminum bracelet with identification disk, individual service record booklet, and a small *Prayer Book for Soldiers*).

Though that already seemed quite a load for one knapsack, the men then strapped various accessories to the outside. At the very top, on the rolled-up blanket placed over the tent canvas enclosing poles, stakes, and cords, would sit an individual mess tin, at a slight tilt to the rear so as not to bump the soldier's head, while at the back of the pack a small bundle of dry wood for cooking supper at the bivouac would be wedged over a stewpot anchored by a strap running up across the mess tin, and from the sides of the pack would hang a few field tools inside their leather covers: ax or shears, billhook, saw, shovel, pick, spade pick, take your pick—along with a collapsible canvas bucket known as the water cow and a lantern in its canvas carrying case. By now this entire edifice would weigh at least seventy-seven pounds, in dry weather. Before sunshine gave way, as it must, to rain.

7

THIS MOSQUITO, at one o'clock, appears in air of a normal end-of-summer blue over the département of the Marne in northeastern France.

Let's propel ourselves up toward this insect: as we draw closer, it gradually grows into a small plane, a Farman F 37, a two-seater biplane carrying two men, a pilot and an observer sitting one behind the other in crude seats barely protected by two rudimentary windshields. Buffeted by the wind, without the shelter of the closed cockpits that will eventually appear, the pair seem installed upon a narrow panoramic porch from which one can admire the landscape of nascent conflict: columns of trucks and soldiers on the move, cantonments and their parade grounds.

And on the ground itself, where all that is crawling

and groaning and the earthbound troops are sweating, it is extremely hot, one of the last heat waves of this mid-August before the swing into autumn takes hold. But high in the sky, where it can be cooler, the men have bundled up.

Underneath their helmets and big protective goggles, dressed alike in leather jackets and trousers, overalls of black rubberized cloth lined with rabbit fur and reinforced with goatskin, plus fur-lined boots and gloves, the two men look all the more identical because their bodies are invisible, aside from their cheeks, jaws, and their mouths, as they try to talk to each other but prove unable to exchange more than poorly articulated exclamations they can hardly hear, deafened as they are by the eighty-horsepower engine, while the brisk air sweeps away their words. The two men seem cast in the same mold, figurines with faintly visible soldered joints, identical lead soldiers except for a brown scarf around the neck of the observer named Charles Sèze, the pilot being Alfred Noblès.

They are not armed, which is to say: not yet carrying the hundred-and-thirty-odd pounds of bombs this biplane can handle; the small machine gun on board is not operational. Although fixed to the fuselage, its design has still not produced satisfactory results—given that it's difficult to aim and reload while piloting, especially since the synchronization gear for firing through the spinning propeller is not yet just right.

What's more, they are not afraid, despite the novelty of this assignment for which they've received barely any training, having been sent on only this one reconnaissance mission. Noblès is at the controls, glancing briefly at the altimeter, compass, speedometer, and inclinometer. Charles Sèze holds an ordnance survey map open on his lap; his brown scarf is entangled with the straps of his binoculars and the aerial photography camera hanging heavily around his neck. As they fly they study the landscape, their only orders being to observe.

Later will come the dogfights and bombing, the no-fly zones over the enemy's territory, the attacks from dirigibles and barrage balloons when things will, and very soon, become immeasurably worse. For the moment reconnaissance is all: taking photographs, reporting troop movements, calculating future adjustments of fire, noting the positions of lines, the capabilities and layouts of airfields and zeppelin hangars along with their outbuildings: depots, garages, command posts, dormitories, canteens.

So they're aloft, keeping their eyes open, when another mosquito shows up way behind the Farman on the left, a new and almost imperceptible insect that neither Sèze nor Noblès notices at first and which, as they have done, will grow bigger and clearer. Wooden framework covered with canvas and adorned with the Maltese cross on the wings, rudder, and the wheels of the landing gear, a fuselage of duralumin: it's an Aviatik biplane making a beeline toward the Farman that leaves little doubt as to its intentions, particularly since as it draws nearer, Charles Sèze spots an infantry rifle protruding from its cockpit and aimed unmistakably his way, upon which he immediately warns Noblès.

We are in the first weeks of the war and the airplane is a new mode of transportation, never before used in a military context. A Hotchkiss machine gun has been mounted on the Farman, true, but as an experiment and without ammunition, so it isn't operational: the use of repeating weapons aboard planes has not yet been authorized by the powers that be, less because of their weight and imperfect performance than for fear that the enemy will take note and arm their planes in turn. Until things change and as a precaution, without paying too much attention to their higher-ups, flight crews do carry along rifles or handguns. Spurred by the sight of that infantry rifle, while Noblès begins evasive maneuvers with the Farman, zigzagging to keep out of the enemy's line of fire, Charles rummages through a pocket of his overalls to pull out a Savage pistol especially adapted for aviation, fitted with a screen to catch spent casings so they won't stray into the propeller.

In the minutes that follow, without losing sight of each other, the Aviatik and the Farman will fly over, pass, avoid, and close in on each other almost to the point of touching, a dry run of what will become the main maneuvers of aerobatics—loop, roll, spin, humpty-bump, Immelmann—with each plane looking to feint while at the same time seeking the best angle of attack to achieve a ballistic advantage. Charles is crouched in his seat, both hands on the pistol grip to steady his gun, unlike the enemy observer, who constantly reorients the barrel of his rifle. When Noblès suddenly sends his plane climbing into the sky, the Aviatik keeps close on his tail, slipping suddenly under him to climb again abruptly while turning, thus targeting the Farman while hiding the Aviatik from Charles behind his own pilot, leaving him helpless. A single shot then sounds from the artillery rifle: a bullet travels 40 feet through the air at 3,280 feet per second at an altitude of 2,300 feet to enter the left eye of Noblès and exit above his nape, behind his right ear and then the Farman, now beyond his control, remains for a moment on its flight path before heading down at an increasingly steep angle as Charles, gaping over Alfred's slumped shoulder, sees the ground on which he will crash approaching at tip-top speed, offering not a hint of hope for any alternative save his imminent and permanent death—ground currently occupied by Jonchery-sur-Vesle, a pretty village in the Champagne-Ardenne region, and whose inhabitants are called Joncaviduliens.

8

WHEN THE RAIN BEGAN, the knapsack almost doubled in weight and there was a mass uprising of stormy wind so deeply frozen that the men wondered how it could even blow: it was perishingly cold when they reached the Belgian border where the customs officials, on the day of the mobilization, had lighted a great bonfire they'd kept going ever since, and around which the troop tried to huddle tightly in an effort to get some sleep. Anthime envied those customs fellows, the tranquil life he assumed they led, their jobs he was sure were safe, and their sheepskin sleeping bags. He envied them again and even more after leaving the village, another two days of marching later when he began to hear the big guns, closer and closer, a basso continuo accompanied by scattered shooting that probably meant skirmishes between patrols.

It was shortly after encountering this battlefront echo that the troop was suddenly sent right into the line of fire, in some foothills a little beyond the Belgian village of Maissin. Now there was no other option: that's when they really understood they had to fight, had to go into battle for the first time, but until a shell actually landed near him, Anthime had not truly believed it. Once compelled to believe it, he discovered that everything he carried had grown heavier: knapsack, weapons, even the signet ring on his little finger, which was now deadweight and had no power to prevent the return, more painful than ever, of the ache in his wrist.

Then orders were shouted for them to advance. Essentially pushed forward by the others, he wound up without much knowing what to do in the middle of a battlefield that couldn't have been more real. He and Bossis looked at each other; behind them Arcenel was adjusting a strap, and Padioleau was blowing his nose, but his face had turned whiter than his hankie. At that point, there was nothing for it, they had to advance on the double while behind them, a group of about twenty men gathered in a circle as calmly as you please without seeming to take any notice of the shelling. It was the regimental band, whose conductor, white baton in hand, brought it down to conjure up "La Marseillaise," aiming to provide valiant commentary on the assault. The enemy had taken up strong defensive positions concealed in a wood, so the men had trouble advancing at first, but when the artillery behind the troop joined the fray to weaken the foe the men tried again to attack, running clumsily hunched over, hampered by their impedimenta, each man leading with his bayonet and spearing the frozen air before him.

As it happened they charged too soon, compounding the error by massing on the road that ran through the combat theater. Open and thoroughly familiar to the enemy artillery set up behind the trees, this road was in fact a perfectly clear target, and right away a few men not far from Anthime set about falling. He thought he saw two or three great spurts of blood but shoved them vigorously out of his mind, not being even certain, not having had time to be certain, that it was blood under arterial pressure—or even that he'd ever really seen blood until then, at least not in that way or that form.

Besides his mind wasn't in good shape for thinking, only for trying to shoot at whatever seemed hostile and above all for hunting down some possible cover wherever it might be. Luckily, although the road immediately received a proper drubbing from enemy fire, it did have low-lying areas here and there where the men had at first been able to seek shelter for a short while.

But for too short a while: barked orders prodded the first lines of infantry off the road and into the oat field alongside it where they were clearly at risk and now, not content with taking fire from the enemy, the men began receiving it as well in the back from the imprudent shooting of their own forces, after which disorder spread swiftly through the ranks. The thing is, they were green troops, and the foul-ups were just beginning; only later would the men be ordered to sew a large white rectangular patch on the backs of their greatcoats, to make them more visible to the observing officers and minimize such blunders. Meanwhile, as the band played its part in the engagement, the baritone sax was shot in the arm and the trombone fell gravely wounded; the group closed ranks and although their circle was reduced, kept playing without missing a note and then, when they began to reprise the measure in which "the bloody standard is raised," the flute and tenor sax fell down dead.

The artillery having come to the company's aid too late in their advance, the troop had been unable to gain the advantage all day, constantly moving forward only to retreat right away. Finally, at dusk, with a last effort they managed to drive the enemy back beyond the woods with a bayonet charge: Anthime saw—thought he saw—men stabbing other men right before his eyes, then firing their weapons to retrieve the blades from the flesh via the recoil. Clutching his rifle, he himself now felt ready to stab, impale, transfix the slightest obstacle, the bodies of men, of animals, tree trunks, whatever might present itself: a fleeting state of mind yet absolute, blind, excluding all others, but in the event the opportunity never arose. He continued to advance with all the others, laboriously, without lingering over the details, but the ground thus gained did not remain that way for long: the company had to withdraw almost immediately, since their position was not tenable without reinforcements that did not arrive. All this Anthime put together only later, when it was explained to him, for at the time he hadn't understood a thing, which is par for the course.

So this was the first taste of combat for him and the others, at the end of which Captain Vayssière, an adjutant, and two quartermaster sergeants were found among the few dozen dead, not to mention the wounded, hastily removed by stretcher bearers just after nightfall. The band had suffered further casualties: one of the clarinetists had been gutshot, the bass drummer and his instrument had been sent tumbling by a bullet through his cheek, and the second flutist had lost half a hand. Picking himself up again when it was all over, Anthime noticed that his mess tin and stewpot had been shot through, and his kepi as well. Shrapnel had torn away the entire bottom of Arcenel's knapsack, in what remained of which he'd found a projectile that had ripped his jacket on the way in. After roll call it turned out that the company was missing seventy-six men.

Leaving at dawn the next morning, the survivors had a lot more marching to do, often through forests where they were less exposed to the enemy's binoculars and aerial observation from aviators and observers in barrage balloons, although the often uneven terrain made progress more difficult and tiring. They were finding more and more corpses, abandoned weapons and equipment; on two or three occasions they had to fight again, but fortunately only in brief affrays that were even more chaotic but in any case less bloody than the first engagement at Maissin.

This slog lasted all autumn and became so routine that by the end they'd practically forgotten they were marching. Which wasn't that bad, after all, one kept busy that way: the body mechanically set in motion left one free to think about something else or more often plain nothing, but the procession had to halt when the war seized up in the winter. What with all this advancing against one another until both sides found themselves unable to extend their positions, it had to happen: everything froze in a standoff during a serious cold snap, as if troop movements had suddenly congealed all along the great line from Switzerland to the North Sea. It was somewhere along this line that Anthime and the others found themselves paralyzed, bogged down in a vast network of line trenches tied together by communication trenches. This whole system, in principle, had been initially dug out by the army engineers, but also and above all by the soldiers, since the spades and picks they bore on their backs weren't there just for show. And as time passed, by trying every day to kill the maximum possible of those across the way plus crawl forward the minimum number of yards the high command required, that's where they plowed themselves under.

9

AT THE END OF JANUARY, as expected, Blanche brought
a child into the world, a female, seven pounds and fif-
teen and two-thirds ounces, first name Juliette. Lack-
ing a legal father—a lack all the more up in the air in
that this presumed-by-everyone biological father had
crashed almost six months earlier just outside Jonchery-
sur-Vesle—she received her mother's family name. So:
Juliette Borne.

That the mother had had a child outside of wed-
lock did not cause much scandal or even provoke excessive gossip. The Borne family was not particularly
straitlaced. For six months Blanche simply stayed home
for the most part and then, after the birth, the war
was blamed for the wedding having been postponed,
Blanche acquired an engagement in public that had

never privately taken place, and the infant's illegitimacy was obscured by the swiftly heroized figure of the supposed father, wreathed in bravery and, thanks to the hurried efforts of Monteil, decorated posthumously with a medal. Even though Blanche's father, thinking of the long term, regretted in his heart of hearts that without a male heir, the future of the factory was not assured, Juliette's birth did not prevent this child, fatherless even before her birth, from immediately becoming the apple of all eyes.

I'll never forgive myself, sighed Monteil; I'll never get over this. The family had indeed hoped, thanks to the doctor's connections, that by dodging the front Charles would be less exposed to enemy fire in the air than on the ground. The connections had worked, of course; everything had gone well: he'd been exempted from ground combat and reassigned to the newborn aviation corps—which no civilian could have imagined then would ever play an active role in combat—as if it were a cushy berth. Whereas that turned out to be a miscalculation: Juliette's putative father disappeared even more swiftly from the sky than he might perhaps have done from the mud. I'll always blame myself for this, Monteil continued. Maybe he would have been better off in the infantry, after all. We had no way of knowing. Blanche replied briefly that regrets were useless, no point in going on and on about it, and it mightn't be such a bad idea if he would instead take a look at Juliette.

Who was three months old, it was the beginning of spring, and Blanche could see things budding in the trees—trees still bereft, however, of even the tiniest bird—through the window next to which she had parked the baby carriage. Forgive me, said Monteil, heaving himself heavily out of his armchair to remove the child from her carriage and examine her—respiration, temperature, alertness—and then declare that my word, she seems to be doing very nicely. Good, Blanche said to him in thanks as she rewrapped the infant. And your parents, Monteil inquired. They're holding up well, said Blanche; it was hard after Charles died, but the child provides a distraction for them. Yes, Monteil began to ramble on again, I'll be angry with myself forever for what I did but it was for his own good, wasn't it. Couldn't be helped, said Blanche firmly. And his brother, aside from that, asked Monteil. Excuse me, said Blanche, whose brother? Charles's brother, Monteil prompted her, have you any news? Postcards, replied Blanche, he sends them regularly. And even a letter, from time to time. At the moment, I think they're in the Somme, he's not complaining very much. That's fine, then, observed Monteil. Anyway, Blanche reminded him, he's never been one for complaints, Anthime. You know how he is: he always adapts.

I O

AS A MATTER OF FACT, Anthime had adapted. What's
more, even if he hadn't, if he'd obviously been having
trouble dealing with things and tried to tell anyone,
postal censorship wasn't a big help to anyone trying to
carp. Yes, Anthime got used fairly quickly to the daily
chores of cleaning, digging and earthwork maintenance,
the loading and transportation of materials, as well as
the periods in the trenches, the shifts of guard duty
at night, the days off. These last existed in name only,
moreover, consisting of drilling, instruction, maneuvers, typhoid vaccinations, showers when all was going well, march pasts, parades under arms, ceremonies
such as the awarding of the Croix de Guerre, invented
six months earlier, or, for example, the recent presenta-
tion to a sergeant major in the platoon of a citation for

devotion to duty at the front in spite of his rheumatism. Anthime had also grown used to the relocations, the changes in the uniforms, and above all, the others.

The others were mostly but not simply peasants, agricultural laborers, craftsmen, and homeworkers, a basically proletarian population in which those who knew how to read, write, and count, like Anthime Sèze, were both in the minority and in a position to help their comrades compose letters or read those they received. The news in this mail was then passed on to anyone interested, although Anthime had kept mum upon learning of Charles's death, sharing this only with Bossis, Arcenel, and Padioleau. Somehow, the four of them always managed in spite of all the troop movements to wind up not too far from one another.

As for changes in the uniforms, it was in the spring that new greatcoats were issued in a light blue that proved quite becoming in the newly returned sunshine. The overly garish red pants had almost disappeared, either covered by blue overalls or replaced by velvet trousers. In the defensive accessories department, the men first received cervelières, close-fitting steel skullcaps, to be worn under the kepi, while a few weeks later, in May, appeared the first sign of a not-so-jolly technological innovation: gags and goggles with mica lenses were distributed to every soldier for protection against combat gases.

Uncomfortable, always sliding off, the migraine-provoking cervelière was not a huge success; more and more of the men stopped wearing them and soon used them only for culinary ends, for cooking up an egg or as an extra soup bowl. It was in the early days of September, after the Ardennes and the Somme,[9] when Anthime's company had moved back toward the northeastern province of Champagne, that this skullcap was replaced by a helmet meant to provide more serious protection, yet initially painted bright blue. Putting them on, the men found it funny not to recognize one another, for the helmets obscured much of their faces. When everyone stopped laughing and realized that sunlight reflecting off this fetching blue made them all attractive targets, they slathered the helmets with mud the way they'd done with the mess tins the year before. Anyway, whatever their color, the men were not half pleased to have them during the fall offensive. Especially on one difficult day at the end of October, when wearing a helmet was no laughing matter.

That day, brutal shelling had begun in the early morning: at first the enemy had sent over only large-caliber shells, well-aimed 170s and 245s that pummeled the earth deep into the lines, shaking loose landslides that buried the wounded and able-bodied alike, quickly stifling them in avalanches of dirt. Anthime almost didn't make it out of a hole that suddenly fell in on him after a bomb landed. Escaping hundreds of bullets whizzing by barely a few feet from him and dozens of shells within a fifty-yard radius, jumping this way and that in the hail of debris, he thought at one point he was done for when a percussion-fuse shell fell quite close to him, landing in a breach of his trench they'd plugged with bags of earth, one of which, sliced open and hurled through the air by the shell's impact, almost knocked him senseless but—luckily—shielded him from the shrapnel. Taking advantage of the general fear and chaos thus sown throughout the network, the enemy infantry chose that moment to attack en masse, terrifying the entire troop into fleeing panic-stricken toward the rear lines screaming that the Huns were coming.

Dragging themselves on their bellies to the nearest hiding place, Anthime and Bossis managed to hide inside a sap—a narrow tunnel leading out from the main trench—running a few yards below the ground, and that's when the bullets and shells were joined by gases, all sorts of them: blinding, asphyxiating, blistering, sneezing, and tear gases liberally diffused by the enemy with special shells or gas bottles in successive waves and in the direction of the wind. The instant he smelled chlorine, Anthime put on his protective mask and then signaled Bossis to leave the sap and get into the open air where, although they were exposed to projectiles, they could at least escape those even more insidious killers, the particularly heavy vapors that gathered to linger in the bottom of holes, trenches, and tunnels long after their clouds had passed on.

As if all that were not enough, hardly had they clambered from their hiding place when a Nieuport biplane fighter, one of their own, picked that moment to crash and explode near the shelter,[10] hurling wreckage all over the trench and intensifying a cataclysm of dust and smoke—through which Anthime and Bossis could see the incineration of two airmen killed on impact and still strapped in, transformed into sizzling skeletons hanging by their seat straps. Meanwhile, although unnoticed amid this turmoil, daylight was failing, and when the sun actually went down a relative calm seemed to return for a moment. But it seemed as well that the desired conclusion to the day would be a last display, a final burst of fireworks, for a gigantic bombardment began again, leaving Anthime and Bossis once more covered in dirt from a fresh explosion when a shell landed on the tunnel they'd only just left, which caved in as they watched.

The shelling died down that night, which might almost have allowed them to rest, if they hadn't had to go all the way to Perthes in the dark through three miles of communication trenches to look for provisions, their supply deliveries having been disrupted by the offensive. Upon his return, Anthime had just enough time before going to sleep to find a letter from Blanche waiting for him with news of Juliette—a second tooth—and to learn from a quartermaster sergeant that the 120th had taken two trenches on the right. On the left, toward the butte at Souain, those across the way had also taken two that had supposedly been immediately clawed back again: in short, no end in sight.

And from the next morning on it went on and on some more, in that perpetual polyphonic thunder beneath the vast entrenched cold. Big guns pounding out their basso continuo, time shells and percussion-fuse shells of all calibers, bullets that whistle, bang, sigh, or whine depending on their trajectory, machine guns, grenades, flamethrowers: danger is everywhere, overhead from the planes and incoming shells, facing you from the enemy artillery, and even from below when, thinking to take advantage of a quiet moment down in the trench, you try to sleep but hear the enemy digging secretly away beneath that very trench, underneath you, carving out tunnels in which to place mines to blow the trench to bits, and you with it.

You cling to your rifle, to your knife with its blade rusted, tarnished, darkened by poison gases, barely shining at all in the chilly brightness of the flares, in the air reeking of rotting horses, the putrefaction of fallen men and, from those still more or less on their feet in the mud, the stench of their sweat and piss and shit, of their filth and vomit, not to mention that pervasive stink of dank, rancid mustiness, when in theory you're out in the open air at the front. But no: you even smell of mold yourself, outside and in, inside yourself, you, dug in behind those networks of barbed wire littered with putrefying and disintegrating cadavers to which sappers sometimes attach telephone cables, because sappers don't have it easy. They sweat from fatigue and fear, take off their greatcoats to work more freely, and might hang them on an arm sticking out of the tumbled soil, using it as a coat tree.

All this has been described a thousand times, so perhaps it's not worthwhile to linger any longer over that sordid, stinking opera. And perhaps there's not much point either in comparing the war to an opera, especially since no one cares a lot about opera, even if war is operatically grandiose, exaggerated, excessive, full of longueurs, makes a great deal of noise and is often, in the end, rather boring.

11

ONE FOLLOWING MORNING, much like the others, snow decided to fall along with the shells—at a different rhythm, naturally, for the shells had been less plentiful than usual, only three so far that day—whereas Padioleau decided to complain.

I'm hungry, Padioleau was moaning, I'm cold, I'm thirsty and also I'm tired. Well sure, said Arcenel, just like the rest of us. But I feel very low, too, continued Padioleau, plus I've got a stomachache. It'll pass, your stomachache, predicted Anthime, we've all got one, more or less. Yes but the worst part, insisted Padioleau, it's that I can't figure out if I feel low because of the stomachache (You're beginning to piss us off, observed Bossis) or if I've a stomachache because I feel low, if you see what I mean. Fuck off, announced Arcenel.

That's when the first three shells that had flown too far, exploding uselessly behind the lines, were followed by a fourth and more carefully aimed 105-millimeter percussion-fuse shell that produced better results in the trench: after blowing the captain's orderly into six pieces, it spun off a mess of shrapnel that decapitated a liaison officer, pinned Bossis through his solar plexus to a tunnel prop, hacked up various soldiers from various angles, and bisected the body of an infantry scout lengthwise. Stationed not far from the man, Anthime was for an instant able to see all the scout's organs— sliced in two from his brain to his pelvis, as in an anatomical drawing—before hunkering down automatically and half off balance to protect himself, deafened by the god-awful din, blinded by the torrent of rocks and dirt, the clouds of ash and fine debris, vomiting meanwhile from fear and revulsion all over his lower legs and onto his feet, sunk up to the ankles in mud.

After that everything seemed just about over. As the smoke and dust gradually cleared from the trench, a kind of quiet returned, even though other massive detonations still sounded solemnly all around but at a distance, as if in an echo. Those who'd been spared stood up fairly spattered with bits of military flesh, dirt-crusted scraps rats were already snatching off them and fighting over among the bodily remains here and there: a head without its lower jaw, a hand wearing its wedding ring, a single foot in its boot, an eye.

So silence seemed intent on returning—when a tardy piece of shrapnel showed up, from who knows where and one wonders how, as clipped as a postscript: an iron fragment shaped like a polished Neolithic ax, smoking hot, the size of a man's hand, fully as sharp as a large shard of glass. Without even a glance at the others, as if it were settling a personal score, it sped directly toward Anthime as he was getting to his feet and, willy-nilly, lopped off his right arm clean as a whistle, just below the shoulder.

Five hours later, everybody at the field hospital congratulated Anthime, showing him how they envied him this "good wound," one of the best there was: serious, of course, crippling, but not more than many others, really, and coveted by all as one of those that ship you away forever from the front. Such was the enthusiasm of his comrades propped up on their elbows at the edge of their cots, waving their kepis—at least those who weren't too damaged to wave—that Anthime almost didn't dare complain or weep from pain, or lament the loss of his arm, the disappearance of which he was not actually fully aware. Not fully aware either, in truth, of the pain or the state of the world in general, no more than he could envisage—looking at the others without seeing them—never being *himself* able ever again to lean on his elbows except on one side. Out of his coma and then out of what served as a surgical unit, his eyes open but focused on nothing, it simply seemed to him— although he didn't really know why—that given the laughter, there must be some reason to be happy. Reason enough for him to feel almost ashamed of his condition, again without fully understanding why: so as if he were reacting automatically to the other patients' applause, to join in the merriment he gave a laugh that came out like a long spasm and sounded like braying, which shut everyone up instanter. A serious shot of morphine then returned him to the absence of all things.

And six months after that, the folded sleeve of his jacket affixed to his right side with a safety pin, another pin anchoring a new Croix de Guerre on the other side of his chest, Anthime was strolling along a quay by the

Loire. It was Sunday again and he'd passed his remaining arm through the right arm of Blanche, who, with her left hand, was pushing a carriage containing Juliette, asleep. Anthime was in black, Blanche in mourning as well, with everything around them blending rather well with that color in touches of gray, chestnut brown, hunter green, save for the tarnished gilding on the shops, which gleamed dully in the early June sunshine. Anthime and Blanche were not saying much, except to mention briefly the news in the papers. At least you've avoided Verdun,[11] she had just said, but he had not thought it advisable to reply.

After almost two years of fighting, with increased recruitment a constant drain on the country, there were even fewer people in the streets, whether it was Sunday or not. And not even many women or children anymore, given the cost of living and the difficulties in shopping, because women received only the wartime allowance at best and in the absence of husbands and brothers, many had had to find work: posting bills, delivering mail, punching tickets, or driving locomotives, when they didn't wind up in factories, armaments plants in particular. No longer going to school, the children had plenty to keep them busy too: much in demand from the age of eleven on, they replaced their elders in businesses as well as in the fields outside the city, where they worked horses, threshed grain, cared for livestock. That left mostly the elderly, the marginal, a few invalids like Anthime, and some dogs on leashes or on the loose.

One of those strays, in the excitement of its sexual arousal by another mutt across the street on the Quai de la Fosse, ran clumsily into a wheel of the baby carriage, which teetered threateningly for an instant until a swift kick from Blanche's high heel sent the culprit off squealing. After making sure that the young woman had the situation in hand and that his niece had not awakened, Anthime watched the woebegone animal—now tacking from one curb to the other, its erection maintained but useless now that its heart's desire had vanished during the carriage incident—until it disappeared at the corner of the Rue de la Verrerie.

12

ANIMALS, WELL, ANTHIME HAD seen a lot of them, of all sorts, during those five hundred days. Because although war prefers cities—besieging, invading, bombing, burning—it is waged in large part in the countryside as well, where beasts are simply a given.

First off, the useful animals: those one works or eats or both, currently abandoned by peasants fleeing their farms turned into combat zones, their buildings ablaze, their fields cratered by shells, their poultry and livestock left behind. In theory, the territorial soldiers were responsible for rounding up these creatures, but that was easier said than done with unclaimed cattle, soon eager to return to a wild state that quickly turned them touchy, especially the bulls, vindictive and impossible to catch. Nor was it a small job for the territorials, even those with a rural background, to gather all the sheep gone roaming along roads in ruins, the wandering pigs, the ducks, chickens, and roosters left to their own devices, the rabbits without any fixed domicile.

These now itinerant species could at least serve, on occasion, to vary the monotonous diet of the troops. Wine was no longer a problem, since it was now widely distributed by the quartermaster corps along with brandy, for the high command was increasingly convinced that inebriating its soldiers helped bolster their courage and, above all, reduce their awareness of their condition. A chance encounter one fine day with a disoriented goose, on the other hand, made a small change from yesterday's bread, cold soup, and tinned beef, and every animal so recuperated thus became a potential feast. Sometimes, driven by hunger and professionally assisted by Padioleau, who enjoyed exercising his butchering skills, Arcenel and Bossis would even carve a few ribs out of a living ox, then leave him to manage on his own. Foragers went so far as to slaughter and devour without qualm idle, bewildered horses, now deprived of their purpose in life, in any case, and upset at no longer having barges to haul along the canal of the Meuse River.

It wasn't just serviceable and edible animals that the men ran into now and then, however. They met up with more familiar ones as well, domestic and even decorative animals that were even more used to their creature comforts: cats and dogs left ownerless after the civilian exodus, without collars or the tiniest daily guaranteed saucer of food, gradually forgetting even the names they'd been given. There were caged birds as well, household pets such as turtledoves, even lawn ornaments like peacocks, for example, which no one ordinarily eats and anyway, given their lousy dispositions and hopeless narcissism, they had no chance whatsoever of pulling through on their own. In general, the military did not spontaneously come up with the idea of dining off that last category of animals, at least in the beginning. It might so happen, though, that soldiers would decide to keep one for company, sometimes for only a few days, and adopt a cat they found wandering in a communication trench as a company mascot.

On the other hand, cavorting around or burrowed

in outside the fixed, static, bogged-down ground plan of the trenches, there were wild animals too, and that was an entirely different business. Before the fields and forests had been razed and smashed to pieces by artillery fire—the fields turned to Martian deserts, the woods reduced to ragged stumps—they had harbored, at least for a little while longer, freelance animals never enslaved by men either in peacetime or in war, at liberty to live as they pleased, unfettered by any code of labor. Among these creatures a decent crop of edible bodies was still available: hares, deer, or wild boar—promptly shot even though hunting was strictly forbidden during wartime, polished off à la bayonet, chopped up with an ax or trench knife—that sometimes provided soldiers with a windfall of alimentary extras.

The same thing happened to birds or frogs, tracked and harvested during the soldiers' off-hours, and to every kind of trout, carp, tench, and pike they fished for with grenades whenever encamped beside running water, and to bees if by some miracle they found a hive not yet completely deserted. Last on the list came the marginal creatures, declared inedible by some vague interdict or other, such as foxes, crows, weasels, moles: as for them, although they were for obscure reasons pronounced unfit for consumption, it seems the troops became less and less finicky in this regard and that every once in a while they managed, by means of a ragout, to make an exception for hedgehogs. Like the other animals, however, these would soon become scarce on the ground after the invention and swift application of poison gases throughout the theater of operations.

But there's more to life than eating. Because in the case of armed conflict, the animal kingdom provides some members that can be too useful as potential warriors to be eaten and these are recruited by force for their aptitude for service, such as militarized horses, dogs, or pigeons: some beasts are ridden by noncoms or set to pulling wagons, others are trained to attack, or haul machine guns, while in the bird department, squadrons of globe-trotting pigeons are promoted to the rank of courier.

Last of all and alas, above all, came innumerable creatures of the tiniest size and most redoubtable nature: all sorts of die-hard parasites that, not content with offering no nutritional value whatsoever, on the contrary themselves feed voraciously on the troops. First in line, the insects: fleas, bedbugs, mosquitoes, gnats, and flies that settle in clouds on the eyes—those choice bits—of corpses. And let's not forget that parasitic arachnid, the tick. Still, the men could have coped with them all, but there was one adversary that quickly became a perpetual and utter scourge: the louse. A prolific champion, this insect in its fraternity of millions soon completely covered everybody. The other main enemy was the rat, no less gluttonous and just as omnipresent as the louse, equally expert at reproduction, but a specialist in fattening up, hell-bent on devouring the soldiers' provisions—including those hung preventively from a nail—or nibbling on leather straps, attacking even your shoes and your very body when you're asleep, and fighting with the flies for your eyeballs when you're dead.

Even if it were simply on account of those two, the louse and the rat, obstinate, meticulous, organized, as single-minded as monosyllables, both of them focused exclusively on tormenting your flesh or sucking your blood, on exterminating you each in its own style— and let's not forget the enemy across the way, devoted through other means to the same end—you often just wanted to get the fuck on out of camp.

Well, you don't get out of this war like that. It's simple: you're trapped. The enemy is in front of you, the rats and lice are with you, and behind you are the gendarmes. Since the only solution is to become an invalid, you're reduced to waiting for that "good wound," the one you wind up longing for, your guaranteed ticket home (vide Anthime), but there's a problem: it doesn't depend on you. So that wonder-working wound, some men tried to acquire it on their own without attracting too much attention, by shooting themselves in the hand, for example, but they usually failed and were confronted with their misdeed, tried, and shot for treason. Mowed down by your own side rather than asphyxiated, burned to a crisp, or shredded by gas, flamethrowers, or shells—that could be a choice. But there was also blowing your own head off, with a toe on the trigger and the rifle barrel in your mouth, a way of getting out like any other—that could be a choice too.

13

IT SEEMS ARCENEL FOUND a third solution, without truly choosing it, actually; there was no premeditation, just an impulse, a mood, producing in turn a moment of pique and then—motion. It all began at the end of December, with Bossis dead and Anthime evacuated, when Arcenel could not find Padioleau either. He looked for him, inquired about him as best he could, even tried to question imperious, contemptuous, tight-lipped officers, all in vain. Arcenel faced the inevitable. Maybe Padioleau had died on the same day as Bossis, buried anonymously in mud without anyone caring or noticing in the confusion. Perhaps he'd been wounded like Anthime, sent home like him without anyone taking the trouble to inform his comrades—or just maybe, who knows why, he'd been reassigned to another company.

Be that as it may, there was no trace of Padioleau.
Thus deprived of his three pals, Arcenel began to feel
fed up. The war was no joke, of course, but it had been
just about livable with the four of them when they'd at
least been able to get together and talk among themselves, trade points of view, argue so they could make
peace again. They'd never wanted to imagine their reas-
suring bond could possibly be severed, in spite of the
increasingly obvious danger everywhere. The thought
had vaguely occurred to them, true, but they hadn't really prepared themselves to see their group broken up,
dispersed, and had taken no social precautions, never
attempted to make other friends.

So Arcenel found himself alone. He did try, during
the weeks and months that followed, to fit in better with
the troop, but it was always a little artificial and he en-
countered resistance because he and his three buddies
had been seen as standoffish, so the others now took
revenge by ignoring him, although given the harsh con-
ditions that winter, a certain solidarity had in the end
kept everyone together as a company. When spring arrived, however, dragging its feet and with no letup in the
fighting, the usual groups re-formed without Arcenel

finding a place in any of them. That's why one morn-
ing, since they were camped near the village of Somme-
Suippe for a breather before rejoining the front lines,
Arcenel, feeling blue, went off for a walk.

Just a walk, for a moment, taking advantage of some
anti-typhoid procedures. Reporting for a vaccination
booster shot, Arcenel was one of the very first to receive
his, thanks to his prime place in the alphabetical list, so
since everyone was all lined up, discreetly baring their
bums to the needle with a frisson of fear, Arcenel just as
discreetly walked off on the spur of the moment, without any particular plan. He left the camp with an evasive
wave to the sentinel as if he were just going to go pee
against a tree trunk, which in fact he did, while he was at
it, but then he went on. When a path appeared, he took
it simply to see, before turning off onto another and
another without any precise intention, advancing automatically into the countryside without really meaning
to wander off.

Relaxing instead into his appreciation of the bur-
geoning spring—it's always moving to admire the
spring, even when one has begun to recognize the pat-
tern, it's a good way to brighten a dark mood—Arcenel

paid just as much attention to the silence, a silence almost untainted by the rumblings at the front, never very far away, rumblings that this morning even seemed a trifle fainter. An incomplete silence, naturally, not entirely restored but almost, and almost better than if it were perfect because it's clawed by the cries of birds, cries that somehow amplify it and, giving depth to a background, exalt it, in the way a minor amendment gives strength to a law, a dot of contrasting color intensifies a monochrome, the tiniest splinter confirms the smoothest polish, a furtive dissonance consecrates a perfect major chord—but let's not get carried away: let's get back to business.

Some animals appeared, still there, seemingly bent on showing the flag: a raptor way up in the sky, a June bug sitting on a stump, a furtive rabbit, which hopped out of a bush to stare at Arcenel for a second before promptly dashing off, spring powered, without the man instinctively grabbing for the rifle he hadn't actually brought with him, not having brought along even his canteen: proof that he'd never planned beforehand to leave the military zone, being moved solely by the idea of ambling around a little while, abstracting himself for

a moment from the horrific shit hole, not even hoping—
because not even thinking of it—that this stroll would
pass unnoticed, forgetting that the men were recounted
all the time, and the roll call endlessly repeated.

Beyond a bend, the fourth path broadened into a
grassy clearing carpeted with cool light filtered by the
freshly unfurling leaves, a delicate tableau. But on a corner of this carpet were three men on horseback, in tight
uniforms of horizon blue, backs straight, mustaches
brushed, expressions severe, aiming at Arcenel three
examples of the 1892 8-millimeter French service revolver while ordering him to present his service record
booklet, but he hadn't brought that along with him either. They asked him for his serial number and enlisted
assignments, which he recited by heart—section, company, battalion, regiment, brigade—while opting to
meet the gentle, attentive, and deep gaze of the horses
rather than the eyes of the gendarmes. Who did not
bother asking him what he was doing there: they tied
his hands behind his back and ordered him to follow, on
foot, the equestrian detachment.

Arcenel should have remembered about them, the
gendarmes, so hated were they in all the camps, almost

as much if not more than the fellows across the way. Their task had at first been simple: to keep the soldiers from slipping away, to make sure they would go get themselves killed properly. Positioned in lines behind the troops during combat, they'd formed a barrier to break up waves of panic and check spontaneous retreats. Soon they'd taken control of everything, intervening wherever they pleased, maintaining order along all thoroughfares in the confusion attendant on the fluctuating movements of troops, policing the military zones in their entirety, at both the front and the staging area behind the lines.

Responsible for checking the passes of soldiers on leave and overseeing all who tried to cross the official perimeters surrounding military units—mainly the wives and whores attempting for various reasons to rejoin the men, but also (and these met with more indulgence) the tradesmen of all kinds, who, selling everything at sky-high prices, proliferated as eagerly as the other parasites on the infantry's back—the gendarmes also tracked down soldiers overstaying their leave, drunks and troublemakers, spies, and deserters, into which last category Arcenel had just unknowingly and unwillingly placed himself. That's how come, back in camp, Arcenel spent the rest of the day and then the night in the locked pump house for the village of Somme-Suippe, without either bread or water, and appeared the next morning before a court-martial.

Arcenel was pushed more than led into the village schoolhouse, where this improvised tribunal sat in the largest classroom: a table and three chairs, facing a stool for the accused. A creased national flag behind the chairs, a *Code of Military Justice* on the table next to some empty forms. These chairs were occupied by a three-man court: the regimental commander flanked by a sublieutenant and a senior warrant officer, and they watched Arcenel enter in silence. Mustache, erect posture, and cold eyes: to Arcenel these men looked just like the ones from the day before, mounted on their horses in the clearing. Since the hour was grave and the shortage of manpower serious indeed, perhaps it had proved necessary to recruit the same actors for this scene, giving them just enough time to change uniforms.

In any event, it all went very quickly. After a brief summary of the facts, a glance for form's sake at the code, an exchange of looks among the officers, the court voted with a show of hands to condemn Arcenel to death for desertion. Sentence to be carried out within twenty-four hours, the court reserving the right to refuse any appeal for clemency, the idea of which had never even crossed Arcenel's mind. He was returned to the pump house.

The execution took place the next day near a large farm at Suippe,[12] at the firing range, with the entire regiment present. Arcenel was made to kneel in front of six men lined up at attention, arms at the order. Among them, from four or five yards away, Arcenel recognized two men he knew, doing their best to look elsewhere, while a divisional chaplain stood in the background. Between them and himself, in profile, an adjutant in charge of the firing squad was waving his saber. The chaplain did his little job and after Arcenel had been blindfolded, he did not see the men he knew raise their rifles as they stepped forward with the left foot, did not see the adjutant raise his saber, he just heard four brief orders shouted, the fourth being Fire. After the coup de grâce, at the end of the ceremony, the men were ordered to march past his body so they would reflect upon his fate.

14

AFTER ANTHIME CAME HOME, he'd been closely watched during his convalescence: they'd nursed, bandaged, washed, and nourished him; even his sleep was monitored. "They" meaning Blanche in particular, who at first had chided him gently for having grown thinner during his five hundred days at the front, without even thinking to make any allowance for the almost eight pounds a lost arm would represent. Then once he seemed nicely recovered, enough even to hazard an occasional brief smile—although only with the left corner of his lips, as if the other one were linked to the missing limb—and when he was able to live an independent life again at home, Blanche and her parents wondered whatever they would do with him.

Of course the army would pay him a pension but

they couldn't let him lie fallow, he needed an activity. Assuming that his infirmity would prevent him from carrying out his duties as an accountant with the same dexterity, Eugène Borne had an idea. While waiting to step into Eugène's position, Charles had been the deputy plant manager, but his sudden death had left open the question of the succession. Putting off this decision for the moment, Eugène had assembled a kind of governing body for the concern, a board of directors with himself as president, which allowed him to avoid having to take all initiatives on his own and therefore sole responsibility for everything. To these weekly collegial meetings already attended by Monteil, Blanche, and Mme. Prochasson, Eugène decided to add Anthime in homage to his heroic brother and for services rendered to the firm, sweetening the deal with some director's fees. Giving structure to Anthime's life without constraining it, this directorship did not entail much but it was something: he was expected to attend, give an opinion—without being any more obliged to have one than the others were to listen to it—vote, and sign papers without necessarily having read them, a task he swiftly learned to carry out with his left hand. In this regard it did seem that others worried more about his handicap than he seemed to himself, for he never mentioned his missing arm.

If he didn't, it was mostly because he had managed almost too quickly to dismiss it from his mind, except when he awakened each morning and looked for it—but only for a second. Forced to become a lefty, he did so without any fuss: having successfully taught himself to write with his remaining hand—and while he was at it to draw, too, more and more, which he'd never done with his right one—he abandoned without regret certain now impractical habits, like peeling a banana or tying his shoelaces. As regards bananas, never having particularly cared for this fruit (a recent addition, incidentally, at the market), Anthime switched easily to fruits with edible skins. Regarding shoelaces, he did not find it difficult to design and commission from the factory a prototype for shoes intended for his exclusive use, a single pair, at first, until the return of peace brought home men interested once again in lighter footwear, and Anthime's Pertinax moccasin became a great commercial success.

Anthime had also to renounce, whenever he wanted to reflect, wait patiently, seem relaxed, or appear pre-occupied, those classic postures taken by crossing the arms or clasping the hands behind the back. At first he instinctively kept trying to adopt them, remembering only at the last moment that he could not follow through. Once he'd finally assumed the role of a one-armed man, however, Anthime did not capitulate so easily, using his empty right sleeve as an imaginary arm, wrapping it around his left one across his chest or grabbing the cuff firmly behind his back. However assumed this role was, though, when he automatically stretched out his arms upon awakening, he also mentally stretched the miss-ing limb, with a tiny twitch in his right shoulder. Once fully alert, and once he'd decided that the day offered few things to do, it wasn't unusual for him to return to sleep after eventually masturbating, which, with his left hand, had not really posed a problem.

So: frequent idleness, to reduce which as much as possible Anthime trained himself to read his paper with a single hand and even to shuffle a deck of cards before tackling a game of solitaire. Managing at last to hold his trump cards under his chin, it took him a little more time before he risked playing silent games of manille at the Cercle Républicain with other cripples back from the front as well, all tacitly agreeing never to mention what they'd seen. Of course Anthime played slower than the veterans who'd lost one or both legs, but also faster than the gas victims who didn't have cards in Braille. But when players kept offering to help him and then peeked at his cards, he finally got fed up and stopped going to the Cercle.

The boredom of those weeks, the solitude, and then—Anthime had the sudden impression one day, in front of the cathedral, that things might be looking up: as his gaze drifted over the pedestrians and pavement, he distractedly ran that gaze up the length of a cane tapping along the sidewalk across the street and wound up staring at a pair of glasses. Such canes were not yet white, as they would be painted only after the war, nor were the glasses completely black, and they weren't dark enough to prevent Anthime from recognizing behind them the face of Padioleau. Sent home from the front at almost the same time as Anthime, guided by his mother holding on to his arm, blinded by a gas that had smelled like geraniums, Padioleau immediately recognized his voice.

The joy of their reunion did not last long, though. Anthime swiftly realized that without his sight, Padioleau as well no longer had the heart for much of anything. Deprived of his livelihood, never having imagined an alternative to the art, science, and style of carving up meat, Padioleau was reduced to zero, in despair over the absence of any possible vocational rehabilitation, unable to envisage a future or comfort himself with the idea that some people can overcome their handicaps and do so in many fields, even in the most sophisticated professions, where they may even reach the heights of genius—although it is true that among the blind, one runs into more pianists than butchers.

Once these two men had found each other again, they were obliged to try passing the time together. Cards being out of the question for Padioleau, reading aloud from the newspaper having finally lost its charm for Anthime, they once more found themselves seriously at loose ends. Attempting to dispel this ennui, they would often evoke the boredom they'd felt at the front and which, edged with terror, had been frankly worse, after all. They distracted themselves by recalling how they'd come up with distractions, and talked about the pastimes they'd invented in the past. D'you remember? D'you remember?

Arcenel used to busy himself sculpting bas-reliefs from the veins of white stone that surfaced in places from the clay of the trenches. Bossis had taken an interest in creating rings, watch charms, eggcups out of scavenged metals: aluminum from spent enemy shells, copper and brass from the shell casings, cast iron from the lemon and egg grenades. Drawing on his civilian background in shoes, Anthime had begun by cutting laces from abandoned leather straps. Then he'd had an idea and turned those same straps, knotted and furnished with a clasp, into wristbands to which he could attach pocket watches via small loops soldered on at six and twelve o'clock. Believing he'd invented the wristwatch, Anthime had cherished the magnificent dream of copyrighting this invention when he got home—only to learn that ten years earlier, Louis Cartier had come up with the same idea to help out his friend Santos-Dumont, a pilot who'd complained how hard it was to consult his pocket watch while flying.

Yes, they'd had some good times in spite of everything. Even though delousing wasn't heaps of fun, still, between alerts it was always a distraction for the men—albeit a vain and temporary one—to hunt down lice, to pry them loose from their skin and clothing, but that arthropod always leaves behind innumerable and constantly renewed eggs, which in clothes could only be killed by a firm pressing with a nice hot iron, an accessory not provided in the trenches. In addition to learning how to use conventional weapons, they'd acquired practical experience with slingshots, and one of their funniest memories, for example, was of winging tin cans full of urine over the barbed wire to the guys across the way. The concerts given by the regimental musicians had been entertaining in a different sense, and then there'd been the accordion the captain sent someone to buy in Amiens: he'd made sure it was played every evening, and the orderlies and liaison officers had danced to the music. And the days when mail was distributed, whenever possible—they had been fun, because the

men had sent off a lot of mail and received a lot, too, tre-
mendous numbers of postcards but also letters, among
which had been the short note informing Anthime of
Charles's death. And now it was too late for Charles to
take advantage of an advertisement that appeared two
years into the conflict: "*Le Miroir* will pay any price for
photographic documents of particular interest relating
to the war."

15

WE ALL KNOW THE REST. The first two months of the spring offensives in the fourth year of the war consumed vast numbers of soldiers. The army's reliance on mass tactics required the permanent replenishment of large battalions, an ever-higher level of recruitment, and ever-younger recruits, which supposed a considerable renewal of uniforms and matériel—including shoes—through large orders placed with suppliers, from which Borne-Sèze profited handsomely.

The pace and urgency of such orders, combined with the unscrupulousness of manufacturers, led to the production of questionable service shoes. A certain stinginess crept in regarding leather of so-so quality; insufficiently tanned sheepskin was often selected, less expensive but mediocre in terms of thickness and durability, and in other words, pretty close to cardboard. Laces were now square cut, easier to manufacture but more fragile than round ones, and they lacked finished ends. Thread was skimped on in the same way and eyelets were no longer made of copper but of iron—which rusts—of the cheapest kind available. It was the same with the rivets, pegs, nails. Bluntly put, they were slashing the cost of materials without any care for the solidity and water resistance of the product.

The quartermaster corps soon raised an outcry about the shoddy performance of these service shoes, which quickly took on water and buckled, not lasting even two weeks in the mud of the front. Too often, the stitches in their uppers began giving way after three days. Headquarters finally complained; an inquiry was swiftly launched. During a review of the accounts of army suppliers, those of Borne-Sèze were carefully examined—and quickly revealed an extraordinary gap between the army's expenditures for these clodhoppers and their actual manufacturing cost. The discovery of such a gaping margin having produced a fine scandal, Eugène pretended not to know anything about it,

Monteil feigned outrage, threatening to resign, and the company wriggled out of it by dismissing Mme. Prochasson and her husband, who had been in charge of purchasing raw materials: the couple agreed to carry the can, in return for a financial consideration. Everything was finally hushed up thanks to more bribes—Monteil's connections were once again called into play—but in the end Borne-Sèze was unable to prevent the affair from going all the way to Paris, where they were summoned to appear before a commercial court: purely a matter of form, but an unavoidable one. To excuse themselves from representing the business in the capital, Eugène cited his age, Monteil his practice; when Blanche was selected, she proposed that Anthime accompany her, and everyone said yes.

Back to Anthime: after his return to civilian life, he had grown used to the absence of his arm even if, in some vague way, he lived as if he still possessed it: an arm as present as if it were really there, which he actually thought whenever he glanced at the right side of his chest, returning to the truth of its absence only when his gaze lingered too long. Assuming at first that these effects would gradually fade away, he soon realized that the opposite was happening.

In fact, after a few months he felt the return of a right arm that was imaginary but seemed just as real as the left one. The existence of this arm, indeed even its autonomy, became increasingly manifest through various unpleasant sensations: shooting and searing pains, contractions, cramps, itching—Anthime would have to stop short at the last moment to keep from trying to scratch himself—and even the old ache in his wrist. The impression of reality was intense and detailed, even to the perception of the signet ring weighing down his little finger, and the discomfort could worsen depending on the circumstances: moments of depression, changes in the weather, as can happen with arthritis, especially on cold and damp days.

Sometimes this absent arm became even more present than the other one, insistent, vigilant, as mocking as a guilty conscience; Anthime felt he could make it perform important or contemptuous gestures that no one would see. He was perfectly certain that he could lean on furniture with both elbows, shake his right fist, control each finger individually, and he even tried to pick up the telephone or wave good-bye, waving—or believing he was waving—when someone was leaving, which made that person think him rather cold and unfeeling.

As if equally possessed by two opposite certainties and at the same time completely aware of these anomalies, Anthime was afraid that others could see this and that pitying him, no one dared mention it—just as Anthime himself didn't dare confide in Padioleau, who was precisely the only one of his companions unable to notice these problems. Problems that worsened and complicated Anthime's life, becoming so invasive that he could no longer confront them alone, no longer grapple with them without asking for help. He finally admitted his misgivings to Blanche, who revealed that she had indeed seen what was going on and then encouraged him, naturally, to consult Monteil.

So Anthime found himself again in the doctor's office, explaining things to him while pointing with his left hand to his missing right arm the way one points at a silent witness, an accomplice a trifle ashamed to be there—while Monteil, frowning attentively as he listened, stared out his office window at a view in which nothing, as usual, was going on or past. Anthime having stated his case, Monteil looked thoughtful for a while before delivering himself of a little speech. This sort of thing happens frequently, he began, and a great deal of anecdotal evidence exists. It's the old story of the phantom limb. It can happen that the perception and sensation of a lost body part will linger on, then disappear after a few months. But it can also happen—which seemed to be Anthime's case—that this body part reasserts its presence in the body long after its loss.

The doctor then developed this speech in the classic manner by calling upon statistics (the upper right limb is, for eight out of ten of us, the most adroit), historical anecdotes (Admiral Nelson, after losing his right arm in the Battle of Santa Cruz de Tenerife and experiencing the same suffering bedeviling Anthime, considered it proof of the existence of the soul), dull jokes (one places a wedding band on the ring finger of the left hand, which then requires the right one to help remove it: the dilemma of the one-armed adulterer), bloodcurdling comparisons (certain penis amputees have spoken of phantom erections and ejaculations), clinical frankness (the cause of these pains is as mysterious as the phenomenon itself), and perspectives that are both semi-reassuring (it will go away on its own, it usually diminishes with time) and semi-worrisome (although it can also last for twenty-five years, that's not unheard-of).

Oh, by the way, Paris, wound up Monteil, when are you going there with Blanche? And the following week they arrived in the Gare Montparnasse, after Anthime had read every last newspaper on the train. Upon his return home from the front, he hadn't wanted to keep up with the news, or at least hadn't shown the slightest interest in the press—although he would sometimes leaf through a paper on the sly—but now, in their compartment, he borrowed the dailies from Blanche and plunged into the events of the day, focused entirely on the war. We were then in its fourth year, well after the particularly murderous business of the Chemin des Dames, the explosive events in Russia, and the first mutinies.[13] Anthime read about all that with close attention.

Blanche had reserved two rooms at the other end of Paris in a hotel run by some family cousins, so they took a taxi at Montparnasse and, as it passed in front of the Gare de l'Est, they saw groups of men on leave milling about, either arriving from the battlefield or on their way back, possibly drunk but certainly vehement, looking angry, singing songs the couple could not clearly hear. Anthime asked the driver to stop the taxi for a moment, got out, and went over to the main entrance hall of the station, where he watched the bands of soldiers for a few minutes. Some of them were singing seditious songs off-key, and Anthime recognized "The Internationale," which opens martially in an ascending fourth, as do quite a few songs and hymns of a patriotic, bellicose, or partisan nature. Anthime stood perfectly still and his face showed no expression as he raised his right fist in solidarity, but no one saw him do it.

At the hotel the cousins showed them to their rooms, which were across the corridor from each other. Leaving their luggage there, Blanche and Anthime freshened up, then went out for a walk before going to dinner. Later, after each had retired to bed, there was every indication that they would both sleep in their separate rooms except that in the middle of the night Anthime woke up. He rose, crossed the corridor, pushed open Blanche's door, and went in the darkness toward the bed where she wasn't sleeping either. He lay down beside her, took her in his arm, then entered and impregnated her. And the following autumn, during the very battle at Mons[14] that turned out to be the last one, a male infant was born who was given the name Charles.

TRANSLATOR'S NOTES

1. *Euntes:* Some parish priests practiced trades to supplement their incomes, and Raphaël Vanni, the curate at Bourgneuf in the département of Charente-Maritime, produced a line of bicycles named after Matthew 28:19, *euntes ergo docete omnes gentes*: go ye therefore, and teach all nations.

2. *Aures Habet et non Audiet:* Victor Hugo took the title of chapter 2 in book 4 of his last novel, *Ninety-Three*, from Psalms 115:6, *aures habent et non audient*: they have ears, but they hear not. The novel appeared in 1874, soon after the bloody uprising of the Paris Commune, and deals with the equally ferocious Royalist rebellions that began in the Vendée region in 1793, midway through the French Revolution, and spread through twelve of the freshly created western départements of France. When Anthime goes off to war on a troop train to the Ardennes in *1914*, he leaves from Nantes, which was the scene of major military engagements during the rebellion and such horrific Royalist reprisals against the populace that French universities today still debate the issue of *un génocide vendéen*. The excesses of the Terror are well known, but the appalling butchery of these revolts against the

Revolutionary government still inspires revulsion and is the backdrop, perhaps most famously, of Balzac's *Les Chouans* and Poulenc's *Dialogues des carmélites*.

In his description of the alarm bells, Echenoz is making a clear allusion to a similar incident in *Ninety-Three*, the opening of the aforementioned chapter when the Marquis de Lantenac, a Royalist leader who has survived an attack at sea by Republican ships, is cast up on the coast of Brittany. There he experiences the same phenomenon: seeing the belfries of the villages spread out before him flashing white and black, white and black, he realizes that the wind is drowning out their sound. And recognizing the tocsin, he wonders for whom the alarm bells toll.

3. *Iron rations:* For a full illustrated description of these iron rations, including the origins of the terms "bully beef" and "monkey meat," Google "Vivres de Réserve—France's Iron Ration in World War 1," and select the site of that name. The Standard Reserve Food ration included two tins of corned beef, twelve hardtack biscuits, two packets of dried soup, two coffee tablets, and two envelopes of ration sugar.

4. *Albert Herter:* The American painter Albert Herter lost a son in 1918, killed near Château-Thierry while fighting in the American Expeditionary Force commanded by General John "Black Jack" Pershing. In memory of his son, Herter gave *Le Départ des poilus, août 1914* (The Departure of the Troops, August 1918) to France, where since 1926 it has hung in the Gare de l'Est. A fine image of this monumental painting may be seen by Googling "Le Départ des poilus, août 1914 | Clio-Photo" and selecting the site of the same name.

Christian Herter, the painter's other son, became governor of Massachusetts and later served as secretary of state under Dwight D. Eisenhower.

5. bonnetière: The *bigouden*, the elaborate lace bonnet that was the traditional headdress of women in Normandy and Brittany during the seventeenth and eighteenth centuries, is still sometimes worn today on festive occasions. Because of their impressive height, these bonnets were kept in *bonnet-ières*, tall, narrow cupboards with a single door, and they can be well over a foot high. A famous *Paris Match* cartoon by the great Sempé shows a Breton woman sneaking a nip from a wine bottle hidden under the towering lace tube on her head.

6. manille: *Manilla*, a Spanish trick-taking card game, spread in the late nineteenth century to France, where it remained popular until 1940, and it is still widely enjoyed in the northern and southwestern parts of the country. *Manille* is played with a thirty-two-card piquet deck, usually by four players in two partnerships, but two or three players can manage it in a pinch.

7. *Byrrh:* Created in 1866, this French aperitif—a blend of red wine, alcohol, grape juice, and quinine—was particularly popular in France in the early twentieth century. Byrrh was sold in the United States until Prohibition and reintroduced to America in 2012.

8. *Ace of Diamonds:* *L'as de carreau* means "the ace of diamonds," but *carreau* is also the word for "square," so this nickname is a play on words. The other popular name for the knapsacks was Azor, the French equivalent of "Fido," because they were originally made of dog skin.

9. *Ardennes and the Somme:* For hundreds of years the European powers have fought over the strategically valuable region of the Ardennes, although by the turn of the twentieth century the difficult terrain there was considered unsuitable for modern warfare. Nothing daunted, in both world wars Germany struck swiftly through the Ardennes to attack where France was poorly defended. The Battle of the Ardennes (August 21–23, 1914) was one of the opening battles of World War I, while in World War II, the Battle of France and the Battle of the Bulge devastated the region once again. In the Battle of the Ardennes, the French counted on their light, rapid-firing artillery to dominate the small German forces they anticipated encountering in wooded terrain favoring their firepower, but the unexpectedly significant German forces, strengthened by their advanced tactical positioning, turned the tables on the French, who retreated in disorder with heavy casualties and were kept essentially on the defensive until the Battle of the Marne.

The Battle of the Somme (July 1–November 18, 1916), one of the biggest and bloodiest battles of the war, was also one of the most deadly confrontations in history, with a butcher's bill of more than a million casualties. The French and British armies, supported by troops from British imperial territories, mounted a joint offensive against the German army, which had by then taken considerable French territory at great cost to both sides and was pressing France hard in its siege of Verdun. Specifically developed to break the deadlock of trench warfare on the Western Front, tanks were first used in combat by the British in the Battle of the Somme, but by the time the Germans withdrew to their fortified Hindenburg Line, the French and British forces had managed to penetrate only a few miles into German-occupied territory.

10. *shelter:* In the forward trenches, officers often had better quarters than the enlisted men, but even the best dugouts were small, muddy rooms, while others were simply rectangular caves cut into the walls of the trench. Some were cubbyholes that could hold only one man, while deep dugouts

might extend more than ten feet underground, but unless they were raised at least a foot above the lowest level of the trench, they could be flooded with filth and dangerous debris.

11. *Verdun:* The German hope for a swift victory when they invaded France had been stymied by Russian offensives on the east and the French victory outside Paris in "the Miracle of the Marne," the desperate counterattack in September 1914 that broke the monthlong German offensive. After the invaders withdrew to the northeast, the Western Front solidified into a four-year war of attrition in the trenches. Hoping to end this stalemate, the Germans mounted a massive offensive at Verdun, which was now a salient on the front lines, open to attack from three sides. The Battle of Verdun (February 21–December 18, 1916) found the French initially unprepared, but German gains were slowed by French reinforcements, and both sides incurred heavy losses as the German advance bogged down. Partly to relieve German pressure on Verdun, the Allies launched their own offensive on the Somme on July 1, forcing Germany to divert men and matériel there. The Battle of Verdun dragged on until the end of the year, as the French clawed back their lost ground.

Modern estimates put the number of dead and wounded at close to a million men. After eleven months, the longest and bloodiest battle of World War I ended with no real advantage to either side.

12. *Suippe:* Le Cimetière militaire français de La Ferme de Suippe, a French National Necropolis, contains the remains of more than nine thousand combatants killed during both world wars.

At five a.m. on March 10, 1915, the French soldiers of the 21st Company of the 336th Infantry Regiment, exhausted by fighting and losses sustained during two months of fruitless combat in their sector, were ordered to launch a fresh attack on the enemy's position north of the village of Souain. The terrain in front of them was strewn with the corpses of their comrades, cut down by withering German machine-gun fire in several recent abortive attacks or fatally enmeshed in the barbed wire both sides deployed to protect their positions. French artillery fire, intended to soften up the enemy, was instead pounding no-man's-land and its own trenches. A witness would later claim that General Réveillac, who ordered the attack, was trying to drive his men out into the open. The French soldiers refused to budge. (During the ensuing court-martial, one of the defendants insisted that "whoever went over the top would have been literally mowed down by either our fire or the German machine-gunners.")

Incensed, General Réveillac ordered the company commander to submit the names of eighteen soldiers and his six youngest corporals, who were brought before a court-martial. Meeting on March 16 in a room of the city hall in Suippe, the court-martial acquitted the soldiers and two corporals and condemned to death corporals Louis Girard, a watchmaker; Lucien Lechat, a café waiter; Louis Lefoulon, a railroad worker; and Théophile Maupas, a teacher. On the following day, March 17, two hours before the camp was informed that their sentences had been commuted to hard labor, the condemned were shot at the Suippe Farm.

Upon receiving the news of her husband's execution, Blanche Maupas began her long battle seeking justice for the corporals of Souain with great courage and perseverance. In 1934, the four men were at last rehabilitated by the Special Military Tribunal for the Review of Court-Martial Convictions, and their names were cleared.

In 1957 Stanley Kubrick made *Paths of Glory*, based on the novel of the same name by Humphrey Cobb, which told the story of the corporals of Souain. Starring Kirk Douglas, the film was released to critical acclaim but was not shown in France until 1975.

13. *Chemin des Dames:* The Chemin des Dames is nineteen miles long, running east and west along a ridge between two river valleys. "The Ladies' Path" was the carriage road taken in the eighteenth century by the daughters of Louis XV when traveling between Paris and the Château de Boves, but in World War I it lay in a strategic sector held by the French army on the Western Front. Pushing the invaders back after the Battle of the Marne, the Allied armies were finally halted on the ridge in September 1914 in the First Battle of the Aisne River, and by the end of January 1915 the Germans controlled that plateau. The front line remained essentially static—but not without casualties—until the Second Battle of the Aisne (April 16–25, 1917), when in what had been presented as a final French offensive for victory, General Nivelle threw seven army corps against the Chemin des Dames ridge, where the Germans were well dug in and had the high-ground advantage. After twelve days of fighting, the attackers had gained little and suffered such high casualties that the French public, kept informed by the newspapers, was outraged. After the massive losses in the battles of Verdun and the Somme, the toll taken at the Chemin des Dames shattered the morale of the disillusioned French troops. By early 1917, almost a million French soldiers had been killed in the war; those still alive were sick of the suicidal attacks demanded by their high command.

The French Army Mutinies of 1917—the startling extent of which was hidden from the public at the time—began after the debacle of the Second Battle of the Aisne: French troops at the Chemin des Dames had been deserting in increasing numbers, but deserters became mutineers as soldiers refused to obey orders for further futile assaults. Revolution was in the air: Nicholas II, the last tsar of Russia, had abdicated on March 2, 1917, and a month later, units of Allied Russian soldiers among the Chemin des Dames troops were singing "The Internationale." In the end, almost half the French infantry at the Western Front may have taken part in insubordination at some point, encouraged at times by the stunning example of the Russian Revolution, news of which was spread by socialist newspapers and the infantry rumor mills.

14. *Mons:* Mons is the capital of the Belgian province of Hainaut, where the British Expeditionary Force fought its first battle of the Great War on August 23 and 24, 1914, against the advancing German First Army. Outnumbered by three to one, and left vulnerable when the sudden retreat of the French Fifth Army exposed their right flank, the British withdrew in good order for more than 250 miles, hard-pressed by the Germans, all the way to the outskirts of Paris. There, together with six French field armies, they were at last able to reverse the Allies' fortunes at the last-ditch Battle of the Marne and begin driving the Germans back to what would become the infamous trenches of the Western Front.

During the Hundred Days Offensive (August 8–November 11, 1918), beginning with the Battle of Amiens, a series of Allied attacks forced the Central Powers to retreat behind the "impregnable" Hindenburg Line—permanently breached in September—and ultimately to accept an armistice. As part of this offensive, the Canadian Corps of the British First Army fought a number of battles along the Western Front from Amiens to Mons, where a memorial plaque in the city hall bears the inscription: MONS WAS RECAPTURED BY THE CANADIAN CORPS ON THE 11TH NOVEMBER 1918: AFTER FIFTY MONTHS OF GERMAN OCCUPATION, FREEDOM WAS RESTORED TO THE CITY: HERE WAS FIRED THE LAST SHOT OF THE GREAT WAR.

PUBLISHING IN THE
PUBLIC INTEREST

Thank you for reading this book published by The New Press. The New Press is a nonprofit, public interest publisher. New Press books and authors play a crucial role in sparking conversations about the key political and social issues of our day.

We hope you enjoyed this book and that you will stay in touch with The New Press. Here are a few ways to stay up to date with our books, events, and the issues we cover:

- Sign up at www.thenewpress.com/subscribe to receive updates on New Press authors and issues and to be notified about local events
- Like us on Facebook: www.facebook.com/newpress books
- Follow us on Twitter: www.twitter.com/thenewpress

Please consider buying New Press books for yourself; for friends and family; or to donate to schools, libraries, community centers, prison libraries, and other organizations involved with the issues our authors write about.

The New Press is a 501(c)(3) nonprofit organization. You can also support our work with a tax-deductible gift by visiting www.thenewpress.com/donate.